This
Christmas Cracker
belongs to:

_____

_____

For Kathleen and
Evi with love
V.F.
For Rob and Elaine
C.F.

First published 1991 by Walker Books Ltd
87 Vauxhall Walk, London SE11 5HJ
This edition published 2010
2 4 6 8 10 9 7 5 3 1
Text © 1991 Vivian French
Illustrations © 1991 Chris Fisher
The right of Vivian French and Chris Fisher to be identified as author and illustrator respectively of this work
has been asserted by them in accordance with the Copyright, Designs and Patents Act 1988
Printed in China
British Library Cataloguing in Publication Data:
a catalogue record for this book is available from the British Library
978-1-4063-3309-1
www.walker.co.uk

# Christmas Kitten

Written by
## Vivian French

Illustrated by
## Chris Fisher

WALKER BOOKS
AND SUBSIDIARIES
LONDON · BOSTON · SYDNEY · AUCKLAND

It was the day before Christmas and very cold.
The little black kitten was hungry and lonely.
"Meeeow," he said, "meeeow."
"What a dear little kitten," said a small girl. "I do
so want a kitten – can we take him home, Dad?"

"I'm sure someone's waiting for him, Sophie,"
said her dad. "I expect he's going home for tea,
just like us."
"Meeeow," said the kitten, meaning, "no I'm not
and please take me home with you." But Sophie
and her dad didn't understand and hurried away.

Some children were playing in a yard.
"Meeeow," said the kitten, running up to them,
"meeeow."
"Cat," said a little girl and she picked him up.

"Put him down, Rosie," said a big boy. "We're
  not allowed cats here – not even at Christmas."
  Rosie put the kitten down.
"Bye, nice cat," she said.

A shop had shining holly for sale, with Christmas cakes and iced buns and sugar biscuits piled up high. The hungry little kitten stood in the doorway.

"Meeeow," he said sadly, "meeeow."
"No cats here," said a man, "not even a little one."
And he shooed the kitten away.

The little black kitten
jumped on to a window
sill. It looked so warm
and cosy inside that he
longed to be there too.
"Meeeow," he said
hopefully, "meeeow."
A little old lady crossed
the room and saw him.
"What a pity I've got a
budgie," she said, "you're
such a pretty puss," and
she drew the curtains.

It was beginning to get dark. The little black kitten shivered. The wind was blowing harder, and more and more people were hurrying home, carrying bags of Christmas shopping.

"Meeeow," said the kitten, "meeeow."
But nobody heard him, and he had to run this way
and that, in and out of their feet.

The little black kitten crept along the pavement
like a little black shadow.
"Meeeow," he said in a tiny tired voice, "meeeow."
He slipped in between the bars of a gate to look
for somewhere to sleep.
"Woof! Woof!" A dog jumped out and the little
kitten turned tail and fled as fast as he could go.

The little black kitten was running so fast that
he didn't see the sleigh and the reindeer in
the road. He fell right against it, and tumbled
into a heap of warm dry sacks.
He sighed, curled up and went to sleep.

The kitten woke with a start. Someone
was talking in a cheerful, rumbling voice.
"Whatever shall I do? I need just one more
present, but there's nothing left in my sacks."
The kitten wriggled out to look.
"Meeeow," he said, "meeeow."

"Well I never!" said Father Christmas.
"Just the very thing."
The kitten held on tight. The sleigh
flew up, up in the air ... and stopped.

Father Christmas scooped up the kitten, slid down the chimney...

...and tucked him into a small sock hanging at
the end of a small bed. "Happy Christmas,
Sophie!" Father Christmas called and dashed
off and away.

The kitten wriggled inside the sock, and fell on
to the floor with a bump. Sophie opened her eyes.
"What's that?" she said.
"Meeeow," said the kitten, "meeeow."

"OH!" said Sophie. "OH!" She picked up the kitten
and hugged him. "It's *my* little black kitten.
It really is. Oh, little black kitten, will you stay
with me for ever and ever?"
"Meeeow," said the kitten, "meeeow."
And he and Sophie curled up together to wait
for Christmas morning.